Contents

igloobooks

Published in 2018
by Igloo Books Ltd, Cottage Farm, Sywell, NN6 0BJ
www.igloobooks.com

WKT001 1018
2 4 6 8 10 9 7 5 3 1
ISBN 978-1-78670-731-4

Written by Melanie Joyce
Illustrated by Sara Foresti

Designed by Kerri-Ann Hulme
Edited by Caroline Richards

Printed and manufactured in China

This igloo book belongs to:

....

Fairy Stories

igloobooks

The Naughty Unicorn

Fairy Petal and Fairy Rosebud were excited. The Fairy Queen had asked them to look after her unicorn, Star, while she was away. She told them to feed and groom Star, but **not** to ride him.

Star was lovely. He was **silky** and **shiny,** with a pink horn. He nuzzled the fairies, playfully.

He's so sweet,

said Petal.

Surely a little ride would be okay?

asked Rosebud. The fairies couldn't resist.

5

Petal and Rosebud jumped onto Star's back and he let out a loud **neigh.** Then, with a **whoosh,** he shot up into the sky.

Don't go too high!

cried Petal. It was very exciting at first!

Star flew faster and faster.
He **zoomed** over a rainbow...

... but soon he started to show off,
looping-the-loop around the clouds.

Make him stop!

cried a scared Rosebud.
So Petal ordered Star to go
back down to the ground.

7

Star **whizzed** down to the woods below and
landed with a **splosh** in a muddy puddle.

He gave a cheerful neigh,
but the fairies weren't amused.
They were covered in mud,
and so was Star!

8

Petal and Rosebud jumped off the muddy unicorn.
Star **whinnied** and rolled in the sticky mud.

Oh, no!

cried Petal.

The Fairy Queen had returned and the fairies felt nervous.

Petal and Rosebud were sure they were in trouble. But instead of being cross, the Fairy Queen **burst** out laughing.

I asked you not to ride him because he's so naughty!

With a **swish** of her wand, the Fairy Queen made them clean again.

The fairies were very relieved. They decided that next time they looked after Star, they would keep their feet firmly on the ground!

Impatient Poppy

Poppy was a rather impatient fairy. One bright
morning, her big sister Bluebell took her to get
a new wand from Miss Flutter's wand shop.

Hurry up!

cried Poppy.

Bluebell told Poppy to wait, but Poppy was in a hurry.
She was determined to get the best wand in the shop
and she wasn't going to wait around for Bluebell!

At the wand shop, Miss Flutter was talking to a group of fairies.
She explained that it was very important for each fairy to choose
the right wand. Otherwise their magic might go wrong...

... but Poppy wasn't listening.

While her friends carefully looked at the wands on display, she **fluttered** around in a flap, looking for the biggest and **sparkliest** wand. And soon she saw it.

The wand was lying on the counter. Poppy was determined to get it before anyone else did.

She flew over as fast as she could and **grabbed** it.

But someone else grabbed it too, and it was Miss Flutter!

They **pulled** and **tugged**. Miss Flutter was just about to say something when a bolt of light flashed from the tip.

There were sparkles **everywhere.**

CROAK!

The other fairies couldn't believe their eyes.

You turned Miss Flutter into a frog!

cried a shocked fairy.

Poppy felt scared. She didn't know what to do.
Just then, Bluebell arrived at the shop.

18

I was too impatient and now Miss Flutter is a frog!

wailed Poppy.

Bluebell said not to worry and that a little magic would put things right.

Bluebell waved her wand and with a **POP!** Miss Flutter was back to normal.

That was my wand you chose.

20 Fairy Poppy said she was very sorry for being impatient.

Miss Flutter smiled and helped Poppy choose a new wand.
Poppy was very patient. She chose a lovely, sparkly pink
wand that was exactly right for her.

With a little patience,
everything had turned out right.

Daisy Learns to Fly

Daisy and her fairy friends were
having their first flying lesson.

Flying School

**That's it, flap your
wings everyone,**

said Miss Flit.

Daisy tried, but her wings
got tired, and she couldn't
flutter very far at all.

Daisy's friends, Crystal and Lupin, were already
flying over the flower patch. Daisy felt disappointed,
but Miss Flit told her not to worry. She said that strong
wings only came with slow and steady effort.

23

So, Daisy patiently practised fluttering off her mushroom.

Crystal and Lupin, however...

... **whizzed** round even faster.

Your wings will get tired,

called Miss Flit, but the fairies flew up into the trees.

Lupin and Crystal flew very high, very quickly.
Soon their wings began to get **really** tired.

I can't keep flying!

cried Crystal. Before they
knew it, the two fairies
began to fall.

Back in the enchanted grove, Daisy heard a cry. Someone was calling for help, but Miss Flit had gone inside to get some fairy cakes.

Flying School

Without thinking, Daisy **flapped** her wings furiously and flew off into the wood.

Crystal and Lupin had dropped safely into a spider's web, but they were **stuck.**

Help! they cried, wriggling around.

Daisy knew she must fly back to the grove and get Miss Flit.

Daisy fetched Miss Flit and soon Crystal and Lupin were
free from the web. They said they were very sorry
and thanked Daisy for being a hero.

Top of the class,

Miss Flit agreed,
smiling.

Then Miss Flit said they should all sit down
and have some **yummy** fairy cakes and a drink.
Daisy felt really happy. She couldn't wait
until her next flying lesson!

Belle and the Dragon

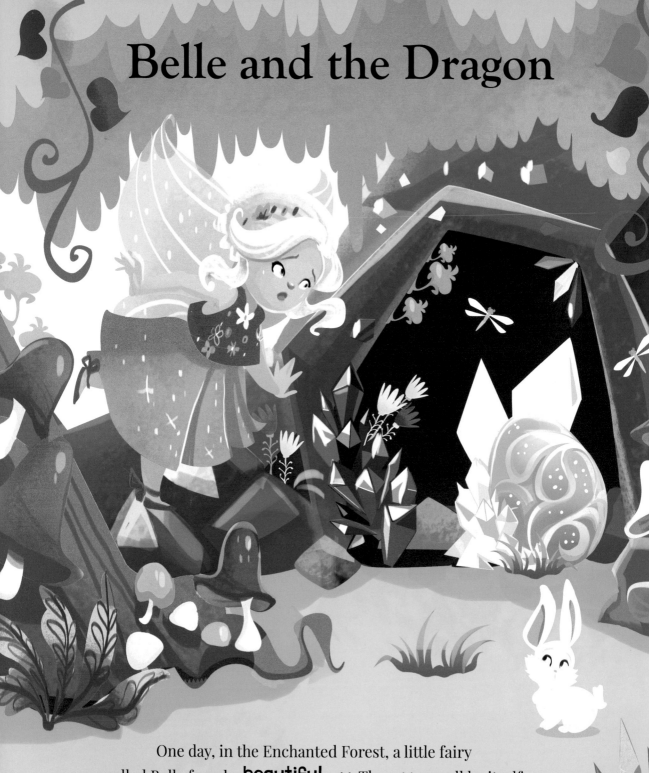

One day, in the Enchanted Forest, a little fairy
called Belle found a **beautiful** egg. The egg was all by itself
and Belle was worried there was no one to look after it.

So, Belle took the egg home and put it on the windowsill in her bedroom.

You'll be safe here,

she said, kindly.

But it wasn't long before the egg began to...

... CRACK!

Suddenly, a baby dragon **jumped** out.

It flew to Belle and nuzzled her. Tiny puffs of smoke curled out of its nostrils.

Oh, you are so cute,

said Belle, giggling.

Belle sneaked outside with her new little friend. They spent ages flying around and playing chase until they were both out of breath.

It was so much fun, Belle never wanted it to end.

Soon, the dragon's tummy began to **rumble,** so they went back home.

You must be hungry,

said Belle.

She tried to give him fairy cakes and acorn milk, but the dragon didn't want them. He didn't want **any** sort of fairy food.

34

Belle didn't know what to do. The dragon was getting more and more hungry. Finally, he let out a little **cry** and flames **shot** out from his nostrils. Belle decided that it was time to tell her mum.

Mum understood that Belle meant to be kind,
but said an egg should always be left in its nest.

The dragon needs
his mummy,

she said. So they both took
him back to the forest.

By the cave was a sad-looking mummy dragon.
When she saw her baby, she **snorted** and the baby
dragon **squeaked** with delight.

I'm sorry,

said Belle, feeling
very sad.

The mummy dragon was **SO** happy to have her little one back that she wasn't cross at all. In fact, every day after that she took him to play with Belle.

There were games of chase and hide-and-seek in
the fairy grove. Belle had never felt happier. After all,
there weren't many fairies who could say they
had a dragon as a best friend!

Blossom's Noisy Bedtime

One night, Fairy Blossom snuggled under her cosy petal quilt
and closed her eyes, ready for a good night's sleep. Just as she was
about to drift off, she heard a loud noise through her window.

Bark, bark!

Outside, the little fox cubs were running round and round the fairy ring, playing chase. They were making lots of noise.

The fox cubs ran off, but Blossom heard another sound. By the fairy pond, the little frogs were hopping across the lily pads, **croaking** loudly to each other.

Feeling a bit annoyed, Blossom politely asked the frogs
if they could croak more quietly. They **dived** into the water...

... splish...

... splash!

There was no more croaking, but now
Blossom could hear **squeaking!**

In the flower patch, the little
mice were playing one last game of
hide-and-seek before bedtime.

I'll never get
to sleep now,

said Blossom, grumpily.
There was just **too
much** noise.

Blossom was wide awake, so she went to get a cup
of acorn milk and sat on her special toadstool. A shooting
star **whooshed** across the sky and Blossom made a
wish for a good night's sleep.

Just then, Mummy mouse called out,

It's bedtime, mice!

The little mice **scampered** off back to their mouse house. There were no more noises to keep Blossom awake, and she gave a **big** yawn.

Soon the tired little fairy was snuggled back under her quilt.

I think my wish is coming true,

said Blossom, sleepily, as her eyes began to close.

The moon shone on the magic wood, and all was quiet and still. The only noise that could be heard was the sound of Fairy Blossom snoring, as she slept soundly all night long!